# Dressing the Monster: Party clothes for the club kid killer

A fashion memoir by Ernie Glam

Copyright © 2018 Ernie Glam

Published by Disposable Fashion Press

ISBN-10: 1986485757
ISBN-13: 978-1986485753

## DEDICATION

To Michael Alig: Thanks for your fun and sometimes uncomfortable inspiration. I'll always love you, except when you waste my time. Air kisses.

# CONTENTS

Acknowledgments i

1 Introduction Pg 1

2 Regressing with kiddie prints Pg 5

3 Are my nipples showing? Good. Pg 8

4 Blood feasts Pg 11

5 Titillating TV Land Pg 14

6 Pearls make everything better Pg 17

7 No pockets in a birthday suit Pg 20

8 Last to get picked for a team Pg 23

9 Star spangled virus Pg 26

10 Crystal Meth Rock Pg 29

11 Games of chance Pg 32

12 Resentful of royalty Pg 35

13 Luring disco dollies Pg 38

| | | |
|---|---|---|
| 14 | Loving the alien | Pg 41 |
| 15 | Instant shows | Pg 44 |
| 16 | Blame the mother | Pg 47 |
| 17 | Willing sidekicks | Pg 50 |
| 18 | The Party Monster wants you! | Pg 53 |
| 19 | Dead eyes | Pg 56 |
| 20 | Outlaw parties | Pg 59 |
| 21 | King of the clubs | Pg 62 |
| 22 | King and queen of New York | Pg 65 |
| 23 | Media hoax | Pg 69 |
| | About the Author | Pg 74 |

# ACKNOWLEDGMENTS

My deepest thanks to Michael Fazakerley, whose collection of club kid portraits from the early 1990s is unmatched. This book wouldn't have been possible without his current and past willingness to collaborate.

I'm grateful to SKID photography/skid@bway.net, David Hurley and KC Mulcare for allowing me to use their photographs.

I also owe much to Thomas Kiedrowski for his proofreading and editorial suggestions.

I'm indebted to the late Alexis DiBiasio, who left me thousands of his club photographs. Rest in peace.

Cover photo: Michael Alig wears a battery-powered LED headband and matching jumpsuit by Ernie Glam. Photo by Michael Fazakerley.

Back cover photo illustration by Ernie Glam.

# 1 INTRODUCTION

Dressing the Party Monster began with an illuminated baseball cap. It was around 1989 at the Red Zone nightclub on W. 54th Street in Hell's Kitchen when I wore a baseball cap decorated with light emitting diodes (LEDs) in the shape of a smiley face.

1989 was the height of acid house, the tweaky British dance music popular at the Red Zone, where mostly college students and young adults hung out. Red Zone was a mixed straight-gay scene and I was part of the club kids, a group of outlandish characters who often worked at the club hosting parties or go-go dancing on the clubs' bars or on tall risers placed at the edges of the dance floor.

The best way to enjoy acid house, in my druggy opinion, was on MDMA, also known as ecstasy or molly. One of the symbols of ecstasy was the smiley face, an obnoxious 1970s symbol often accompanied by the slogan "Have a nice day." Since the acid house trend was well underway when the Red Zone peaked in popularity, smiley faces were on t-shirts and clothing, so I needed something more unusual than a smiley face t-shirt with a bloody bullet hole through the forehead. That meant a trip to Radio Shack for wires, a soldering gun and LEDs to create an illuminated smiley face baseball cap that everyone inside the darkened Red Zone would covet. It worked.

One of the Red Zone's promoters, Michael Alig, saw the hat and immediately asked me to make him one. I made him a hat because he often hired me at Red Zone and I wanted to continue getting gigs there. At the Red Zone he was a zany and playful guy, though Michael would eventually be known as the Party Monster because of his role in the death of Angel Melendez in 1996. After the baseball cap, Michael expressed interest in the clothes I

Ernie Glam, left, as Disco 2000 mascot Clara the Carefree Chicken, with Michael Alig in an assless jumpsuit and matching headband by Ernie Glam. Photo by Michael Fazakerley.

was making and wearing to the clubs. In the mid-1980s I took night classes at the Fashion Institute of Technology to learn the basics of garment design and construction to make clothes I wished were for sale in stores, but weren't. Even if they had been for sale in stores, I probably couldn't have afforded them, so do-it-yourself was the only option.

Conversations Michael and I had about wacky club clothes led me to make him all kinds of garments, like the lamé silver chaps that he wore to an illegal party at a McDonald's with no underwear and just feathers I glued to his penis for "modesty." It wasn't the only time I glued feathers, sequins and other decorations on his cock. To this day Michael is the only man whose penis I've repeatedly handled non-sexually.

When I showed up at one of his parties wearing a yellow jumpsuit with flaps on the rear that were fastened in a way to reveal my ass, he asked me to make him assless jumpsuits. Those assless jumpsuits, which the writer Michael Musto eventually dubbed the new crack epidemic, began a three-year period when he hired me to design clothes for him almost weekly.

Generally, outfits had to be ready by Wednesday afternoon because he often debuted them at his party Disco 2000 in the Limelight nightclub. The garments were intentionally designed to get attention, shock or offend. Combined with Michael's outrageous antics, including behaving as if he was very intoxicated, the garments got him copious attention and photo-ops that appeared in magazines, newspapers and books.

The Party Monster wasn't kind to most of the creations made for him. The illuminated baseball cap should have been a warning to meticulously document my creations. Like other red flags back then, I didn't heed it. Within days the baseball cap was broken. Despite repeated repairs to the hat's fragile electronics and warnings that he be gentle, he kept breaking it. Subsequently, most of the garments I made for him were quickly ruined through the same behavior and antics that broke the smiley face cap. Like Dr. Frankenstein's creation, part of his nature was to simply destroy things. Most of the destruction wasn't intentional; he just couldn't help himself.

I eventually had a bit of forethought and took some photos of my creations. Several friends from the club scene also did and they shared their images for this book. The following photographs, some taken in Michael Fazakerley's studio-apartment before we hit the clubs, document a few of the costumes I designed for Michael before they were ruined in the chaos of the dance floor.

Many of the looks are variations on unitards or stretchy bodysuits, which seem like club fashion staples today, but in the late-1980s these items were virtually impossible to buy in men's sizes. It's satisfying to have watched our favorite garment, the flashy bodysuit, become a club kid stereotype. I don't know if Michael and I can claim any credit for this stereotype—he probably would—but we were likely the first club kids to wear garments like these on national television.

Our fashion collaboration ended around the summer of 1993, when our drug abuse made it increasingly difficult to work together or get along. I moved out of his apartment that summer as part of an effort to dial back the drug use, though it still took another year to fully kick my crystal meth habit. After kicking my habit I kept Michael at an arm's-length distance from 1994 until the time of his arrest. It was only after he was sent to prison that we were able to renew our friendship.

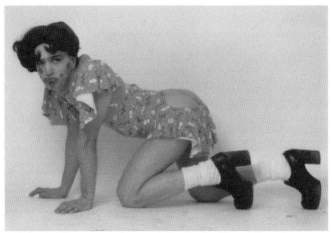

Michael Alig wears a jumpsuit by Ernie Glam. Photo by
Michael Fazakerley.

## 2 REGRESSING WITH KIDDIE PRINTS

In the late 1980s and early 1990s there were many fabric
stores on West 39th and West 38th streets in Manhattan
that sold remnants of children's fabrics, often for 99 cents
a yard or less. It was fortunate that the fabric was so cheap
because at first I wasn't so good at sewing or cutting
patterns, so I'd end up wasting a yard or two through
mistakes.

I loved using the cast-off or surplus children's prints for
our club costumes because they represented our wasteful
and disposable consumer culture. These leftover fabrics
landed on West 39 and West 38 streets in budget fabric
stores that were trying to squeeze one last penny of profit
from them. They were essentially junk fabrics one step
removed from the garbage can, so why not make them
trashy?

Michael Alig wears a jumpsuit by Ernie Glam. Photo by
Michael Fazakerley.

These fabrics never had tags on them stating country of
origin, but it was a good bet they were made in some
impoverished nation by workers paid $1 an hour or less.
That was another element of our mockery. We were taking

fabrics produced through exploitation of foreign workers for privileged American children and re-exploiting the product. Therefore, fabric made through exploitation for innocents got temporarily diverted from the landfill so that it could be briefly re-exploited before it was destroyed in a drunken, high frenzy at a nightclub.

The gender-specific nature of many children's prints didn't matter to the Party Monster. It depended on his mood and the print. He was fond of prints with candy and anything suggesting the carefree happiness that he resented losing in adulthood.

The concept for the pink cotton lycra unitard with fish and waves on pages 5 and 6 was a swimsuit that you wouldn't necessarily swim in because there's too much drag in the tail or because your butt is sunburned. Michael Fazakerley's photo shoot produced a portrait that could be used for the invitation to Michael's birthday party. The shoot captured a number of good poses, but the one chosen for the invite was a head shot like the one on page 6 that was printed on a box of candies tasting like chalky Valentine's hearts.

Michael ordered several thousand candy boxes and we distributed them at the Limelight and elsewhere. His logic was that no one would discard his birthday invite because it contained candy. It was bad candy, but candy nonetheless. So according to his logic, clubbers would at least keep it until they ate all the candies. Then they'd have sugar highs and the party would be imprinted in their subconscious. Doesn't a subconscious become more impressionable when plied with sugar? Free drugs might have had the same effect, but sugar was cheaper.

# 3 ARE MY NIPPLES SHOWING? GOOD.

Dressing the Party Monster called for attraction and repulsion. That meant emphasizing an erogenous zone and then accessorizing it in some sexy way that could also be a turn-off. That was the case with nipples, which we loved painting or decorating with glue and sequins. Our initial assumption was: Who would suck on your nipple if the reward is a mouthful of spirit gum?

It turned out that the answer to that question was plenty of people! The clubs were full of strange partiers who were actually turned on by our sexy subversion. I often had to carry extra sequins and spirit gum, which was stickier than latex eyelash glue. I didn't carry the extras in case I knocked the sequins off my nipples, but because someone would invariably pinch my nipples or try to bite them and then knock sequins off. Despite all this nipple action, it never led to sex because the instigators were usually too drunk to fuck.

In the photograph on page 9, the Party Monster's nipples are accentuated by a Christmas ensemble in red stretch velvet from around 1991. It was a one-piece that exposed both the chest and the ass. White pearls hung near the nipples and over the ass in the back. The concept was an unsexy Santa elf — the kind of elf sent with gag gifts to naughty children and adults. And don't even expect a peppermint candy cane from this unsexy elf, because what you'll get is a pole made flaccid by drugs and tasting like sweaty jingle balls. We set up a Christmas tree that holiday in our apartment and a lack of traditional ornaments led us to top it with a plastic skull and a casually thrown bra. What we didn't anticipate is how many of the tree's decorations would eventually be incorporated into outfits, so by the actual celebration of Jesus' birthday, the tree was half bare—like Michael's ass!

8

Michael Alig wears a Christmas suit by Ernie Glam. Photo by
Ernie Glam.

My recommended cocktail to accompany Michael's Christmas outfit was a Rumple Minz and vodka. Rumple Minz is a type of peppermint schnapps that on its own is too sweet, so the bartender Olympia at Disco 2000 used to cut the Rumple Minz with Absolut vodka. "It's a liquid breath freshener," she said in her gravely voice the first time she suggested one. She was right. It tasted like Scope mouthwash, but it got you way more fucked up and your breath did in fact stay minty fresh no matter how

The bartender Olympia.
Photo by Alexis DiBiasio.

wasted you got. You could force your tongue into anybody's mouth without concern that they'd recoil because of bad breath. If objects of the sloppy kisses recoiled, it was because they were repulsed at the thought of kissing us, but they couldn't find fault with our minty breaths.

This Christmas outfit's mystery was how the velvet crotch stayed fixed around the "candy cane," since there were no visible straps in the back because we didn't want lines across the ass. The trick was a cock ring-like strap that could be fastened around the penis and balls to hold the fabric in place. The elastic strap was flexible enough to easily remove when there was a need for urination. The elastic strap allowed for many Christmas surprises during the night when the Party Monster pulled his junk out of its velvet sack for shock value. Some clubbers might have wished they'd gotten a lump of coal instead.

# 4 BLOOD FEASTS

Two types of blood were spilled at Michael Alig's Disco 2000 party.

Some of it, in small amounts, oozed from drunk people's limbs and bodies when they fell down the ridiculous amount of stairs in the Limelight nightclub. The pleasure palace was an Americans with Disabilities Act nightmare. Originally built as a church, there wasn't a need for many stairs. As a nightclub, however, the architects added various mezzanine levels above the dance floor so that partygoers could watch the dancing or the performances on stage. Those upper levels also allowed patrons to discretely use drugs. There were stairs going to the DJ booth, to the library and to the main bathrooms. Those stairs, combined with the giant platform boots and sneakers that were in fashion in the early 1990s, brought down clubbers at least once an hour at Disco 2000.

Those trickles of blood weren't enough for the Party Monster. He desired larger amounts.

So, he turned to fake blood, which was copiously spilled. Michael was a big fan of Herschell Gordon Lewis' 1963 film Blood Feast, considered one of the first gore films for its graphic depictions of mutilation and evisceration. His fascination with lurid grind house films that could be seen in Times Square theaters in the early 1980s before the area's Disneyfication fueled his desire to make his parties reflect crazed scenes from these movies. At one point he dubbed one of his recurring themes Blood Feast, forcing all of us who worked at Disco 2000 to don horror looks and cover ourselves in blood. That meant I had to create a "blood-splattered" apron to wear on top of my Clara the Carefree Chicken costume. Then I was given a giant butcher knife made by the club's art staff so that I could

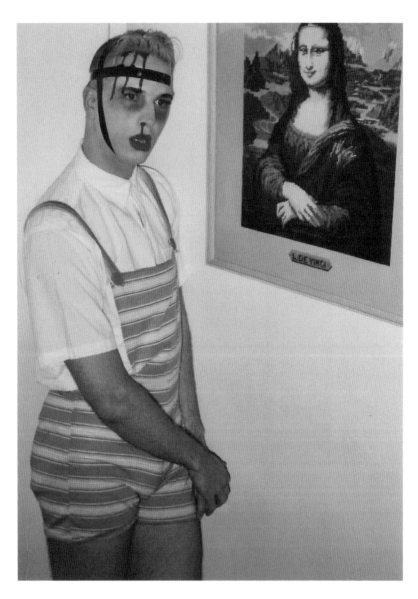

Michael Alig wears a jumper by Ernie Glam. Photo by Ernie Glam.

stalk patrons and pretend to stab them.

The club kid aesthetic cherished shock value, so what better way to shock than with human blood? The goal was to scare or worry our friends and paying customers. Was it real blood? Maybe they went to the Meat Market District and bought some cow's or pig's blood, customers might have wondered. It wouldn't have been beyond the realm of possibility that we bought cow's blood for a party. Others might have thought that the blood wasn't real, but they were wary nonetheless because they didn't want it on their outfits. "Don't you dare come near me," was a threat made by at least a few queens on the Blood Feast nights when I was in character. That wasn't just an idle threat and you'd best know who you can dry hump and who you can't when covered in blood. There was a large contingent of voguing and pier queens each week at Disco 2000, and those mean bitches weren't reluctant to smash a beer bottle and draw some real blood if you fucked up their looks. Whether it was real or fake, clubbers recoiled at the sight of it. And despite the real or fake disgust, each successive Blood Feast theme night drew more attendees.

I can't remember if Michael wore this comfy cotton-polyester knit jumper for one of his Blood Feast themes. Even when it wasn't a Blood Feast night, he was prone to dribbling some blood on himself. This was still the height of HIV/AIDS hysteria, so the sight of blood made onlookers cringe—not for the bloody one's welfare, but for their risk of contagion.

13

# 5 TITILLATING TV-LAND

The club kids' antics at the Limelight nightclub didn't just accidentally attract media attention. The Limelight had publicists on staff to create gossip items for columns like the ludicrous-but-well-read Page Six in the New York Post. Publicity begat publicity, and the short print items of semi-celebrities or fashion designers cavorting with club kids and drag queens at the Limelight eventually attracted the attention of the daytime television talk shows.

Club kids were perfect for trashy daytime talk shows. The club kids' outlandish looks, provocatively queer behavior, hedonism, barely veiled drug use and their disdain for many of the conventions of adulthood, including day jobs, made them irresistible bait for judgmental audiences. Some hosts were decidedly on the hostile audience's side and they did their best to roast the club kid guests, but others like Joan Rivers and Phil Donahue were more sensitive and supportive.

Producers from the Joan Rivers Show came to the Limelight sometime in 1991 or 1992. They came to the Disco 2000 party to see the club kids in action and Michael Alig walked the producers around the party to introduce us to them. I remember one of the producers jaw was basically hanging open as he shook hands. Some of us had been informed of the producers' visit several days beforehand, so I designed an especially wild look for myself involving a fabric "cage" rising up from my neckline and attaching with buttons to a band around my forehead. The look worked its magic and the producers immediately asked me to be on the show.

There was no question that Michael would appear with Joan Rivers, so I designed one of my crack epidemic jumpers for him. The cotton-lycra black and white plaid jumper on page 16 revealed his entire ass and then wrapped around his legs. So when he came from backstage onto Joan's stage it looked like he was wearing a one-piece jumper until he spun around and mooned the audience, which audibly gasped.

Daytime talk shows had the annoying habit of recording their shows very early in the morning, or at least at a time that we considered early in the morning. I believe Joan Rivers' producers asked us to come on a Thursday morning at 8 a.m. Of course we were at Disco 2000 from Wednesday night at 11 p.m. until around 5 a.m. Thursday morning, so we didn't have time to sleep. My solution for the sleep deficit was to snort some crystal meth, which I'm sure was shared with Michael. The combination of sleep deprivation, tweaking and a lack of preparation left us without pithy one-liners we could deliver on camera.

Although we spent days working on Michael's look, we devoted considerably less time to what we would say during the show. Amanda Lepore had a small panic attack while sitting in the green room and we had to walk her back from the edge by reminding her that she should simply say that she's every man's fantasy.

We were also worried that Joan Rivers, known for her acerbic commentary, would wag her acid tongue in our direction. We were surprised to learn that she instantly loved us and I was very impressed with her ability to make our appearance on the show very funny without really insulting us. Backstage Joan Rivers posed with Michael, but not too close because she didn't want his body paint staining her outfit.

Talk show host Joan Rivers, left, and Michael Alig wearing a jumpsuit by Ernie Glam. Photo taken by one of Rivers' staffers with Ernie Glam's camera.

# 6 PEARLS MAKE EVERYTHING BETTER

My designs for Michael Alig weren't always elaborate. In the New York City club kid scene of the later 1980s and early 1990s, clubbers dressed to make statements, and certainly not in subtle ways.

Still, unsubtle statements could be made subtly. For instance, what cleavage isn't rendered more elegant when draped in pearls? Our vulgar club kid twist on pearl-draped cleavage was the pearl-draped ass crack. The goal was to decorate something deemed repulsive by some people with cheap reproductions of precious jewelry. Think about it. Ass cracks are tawdry and so are fake pearls. They're meant to be together.

Pearls were important to the Party Monster because of his fascination with television shows from the 1960s and 1950s, when women wore pearls even while doing housework. On the gothic soap opera "Dark Shadows" the "scientist," Dr. Julia Hoffman, was prone to fingering or clutching her pearls while speechifying on the origins of vampires and werewolves or wondering how to harness the power of the I Ching for time travel. The Party Monster often imitated her when speculating about something.

We were both big fans of Joan Crawford's early 1960s horror movies like "Straight-Jacket," in which several women wore pearl necklaces, including the murderous daughter who chopped up her victims with an axe. I distinctly remember watching "Straight-Jacket" with the Party Monster and laughing wildly. This was years before the Party Monster was convicted of a death similar to the ones in "Straight-Jacket." Readers might wonder how I could remain friends with someone who reenacted part of a horror movie. By the time he committed his crime he'd

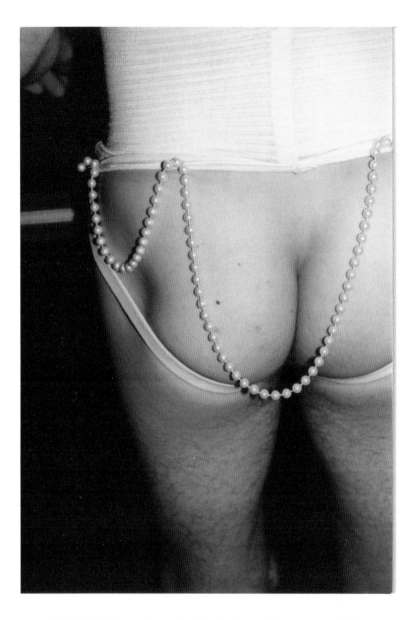

Michael Alig's ass draped with plastic pearls sewn to a girdle
by Ernie Glam. Photo by Alexis DiBiasio.

become a drug zombie and I had very little contact with him. The man released from prison was more like the friend I'd made in the late 1980s and not the drug zombie of 1995.

Wearing pearls on your ass means that at some point you're sitting on them, which negates their precious, decorative value. When seated, they're just uncomfortable little plastic balls that leave ugly, red indentations on your butt cheeks. Frankenstein's monster had bolts sticking out of his neck; the Party Monster had plastic pearls stuck to his butt cheeks. We were trying to degrade the precious while elevating the vulgar. All the better for this anal mash-up if an ass-crack hair plucked from its chasm by the pearl strand got tangled in the strand's cheap, scratchy fibers.

Draping a pearl necklace over the ass crack was our radically queer statement. The outfit on page 18 was worn during the AIDS epidemic around 1989, when many gay men died because science hadn't found a way to manage HIV so that it didn't develop into AIDS. The pearl necklace was a metaphor for semen dripping out of the ass. It was our gallows humor about anal sex, but also a warning, a mockery and a horror show. It didn't occur to us to insert a bunch of pearl strands in the Party Monster's rectum and have a decorative pearl cluster dangling from between his legs like a super-shiny, abundant bloom of dingle berries. I supposed I could still talk him into turning that look, but it wouldn't be as shocking today.

Plastic pearls tend to crack and crush, especially if you sit on them. Broken or crushed fake pearls appealed to me because they vaguely resembled cocaine before it's crushed into a powder. For me, seeing a little piece of plastic pearl embedded in Michael's ass cheek reminded me of the little coke or special K clots that I sometimes saw in his nostrils, another kind of white dingle berry.

# 7 NO POCKETS IN A BIRTHDAY SUIT

Going out almost naked has obvious drawbacks, like no pockets. That's why so many club kids carried lunchboxes. All the makeup, extra glue, keys, money, breath freshener and drugs would leave unsightly bulges in a girdle or jock strap. You really only want select bulges with the near-naked look.

One of the advantages to the near-naked look is that no matter how often you fall down or someone spills drinks on you, chances are high that your look won't be ruined. There's almost no fabric to tear while breaking into a gated park for an outlaw party, especially if the trespass required climbing a fence.

Clown imagery worked well with the near-naked look. The circus and its sideshow freaks were role models for the club kids. If you're going to make a spectacle of yourself, why not smear clown white all over your face and start adding color? And while you're adding color, glue on some sequins and fake eyelashes. Why stop there? Get some fake blood, maybe a latex scar or a plastic bug and apply those too. Once you've done all this, who needs clothes?

For one of the Party Monster's simpler looks like the one on page 21, I affixed spangles to the ends of a pearl strand and glued it on to Michael's chest. The pearl strand draped over his ass cleavage is also partly visible. It was probably summer and clubs got hot, so it was comfier going out almost naked.

On the night I glued the pearl strands on Michael chest I most likely carried a vial of spirit gum in my lunchbox for touch ups if someone pulled the pearls off. He didn't fuss much about his clown makeup. It just got messier as the evening progressed.

Michael Alig wears pearl stickers by Ernie Glam. Photo by
Alexis DiBiasio.

Even with such a no-fuss look, there were perils, especially with lunchboxes. The drawback to carrying a lunchbox is that you'd be so drunk or high that you put it down somewhere, then walked away forgetting it. That only happened to me a couple of times in the clubs, but it was always devastating. One night while hosting a party I put the lunchbox down on the stage for just a second to help someone and a clubber at Red Zone snatched it. It was probably one of those sexy rough-trade Latino guys that used to go there for the acid house and drag queens. Some of them were shady motherfuckers. The most valuable possession in the stolen Hello Kitty lunchbox was about 20 drink tickets, so somebody really had a good time. Luckily I didn't have my wallet or keys in there because my boyfriend lived nearby and I left them at his house.

Yet another drawback is the police. On several occasions cops threatened us with arrest for public indecency if we didn't leave a location or go inside a club. All because our asses were exposed! The unanswered question since we didn't get arrested is the definition of indecency. It seemed very arbitrary that cops would make this threat and then not arrest us. We could have challenged them in court, but who wants to be arrested and miss the rest of the night's party just to prove a constitutional right to freedom of expression in court?

New York City police officers now seem strangely tolerant of exposed asses. Throughout 2017 I saw drag queens and club kids with most of their asses exposed and in many cases these clubbers took the subway to the party! Just don't try to get into the subway by jumping the turnstile, cops still care about that.

# 8 LAST TO GET PICKED FOR A TEAM

Athletic prints or sports uniform fabrics appealed to us because they were opportunities for mockery. Take all that safety gear off the playing field, put it on a dance floor and it's utterly ridiculous. Few high school gym classes wanted us on their teams, so I created a special "varsity" look on page 24 for Michael made from a white football jersey fabric with a giant team letter. No athletic stamina was required for this look, unless you count marathon dancing until sunrise on MDMA.

Ernie Glam, left, holding an Uzi squirt gun with Dean Bowery. Photo taken with Ernie's camera.

The crotch on the "varsity" outfit needed a contrasting fabric for two reasons. The seam in the center of the black-and-white polka dot triangle concealed a zipper that allowed Michael to pee without removing the costume. The other reason was that the "varsity" fabric had little holes and it was slightly transparent, so the opaque polka dot fabric afforded a bit of privacy even if the Party Monster wasn't interested in modesty.

We never played any sports. OK, we played water sports if you count the times the Party Monster sprayed people with his urine while we rampaged through clubland. One night I brought a bright yellow and orange Uzi squirt gun to the Red Zone. Michael asked to borrow it, then went into the

Michael Alig wears a jumpsuit by Ernie Glam. Photo
by Alexis DiBiasio.

bathroom, presumably to fill it. When he emerged he proudly declared that he'd pissed in it. Some of our friends recoiled in horror, but I wasn't entirely convinced that my gun really had urine. What if he was simply saying it for shock value? Still, I didn't know. I didn't follow him into the men's room. Why would I?

At one point it was time to leave. Once outside Michael shed all sense of restraint. He worked at Red Zone, so he couldn't really shoot people with abandon. But once inside a taxi, he pointed the gun out the window and began shooting at unsuspecting pedestrians. It was 2 or 3 a.m., so there weren't too many people on the sidewalks. All the better for him, since at that hour there wasn't much traffic to slow down the taxi, so there was no danger that some angry, wet pedestrian would lunge at the taxi to rip open the door and kick his ass.

I don't remember where we were going, but it was probably another club or party since we never went home after working our shifts at Red Zone. Michael probably sprayed a half dozen people before I decided that it was no longer funny. The last urine drop was when we were paying the taxi driver. One of us handed him them money and then Michael "accidentally" sprayed him while leaning into the front of the cab to give the poor guy his tip.

That was it. After the taxi pulled away I grabbed the uzi out of his hands. We had some scuffle and argument, then I shot him in the face. The tepid stream didn't have a soothing effect. Enraged, Michael scuffled with me some more, ripped the uzi out of my hand and threw it to the ground. He stomped on the plastic toy until is was shattered in pieces while cursing. Apparently he really did piss in it.

# 9 STAR SPANGLED VIRUS

At some point we decided that all garments should have spangles or some sort of shiny, sparkly decoration. The reason why we decided that spangles were the must-have accessory for our costumes is lost in the past. Perhaps we felt that clown makeup didn't have the same impact as in earlier days. Or maybe our feet hurt from the massive platform shoes that always left my ankles sore at the end of the night because they felt like cement blocks. Whatever the cause, we launched a love affair with spangles.

Usually the spangles were sewn around the cuffs of long sleeves or the neckline, as is the case with the white and black polka dots, cotton-lycra bodysuit on page 27. Call the ensemble an attempt at pretty. What could be more lovely than a tweaked-out Party Monster at 4 a.m. with spangles flashing from his wrists as he raced around the Limelight nightclub with a bottle of vodka forcing all his friends to take a swig?

The vodka bottle gulp was a regular game at the Limelight in the pre-dawn hours after the bars in the club closed. Michael would "steal" a bottle from behind one of the bars and then run around triumphantly offering swigs. Of course there were lots of takers. Nobody wanted the party to end, the crystal meth hadn't worn off, somebody wasn't drunk enough. There were all kinds of reasons why someone wanted a swig.

Disgusted by the communal sippy cup, I often ran in the opposite direction when I saw Michael approaching with a bottle. Even if you waved your hands emphatically indicating that you were not thirsty or in the mood, he'd try to press the mouth of the bottle against your lips to force you to join in the party.

Michael Alig wears a spangled jumpsuit by Ernie Glam. Photo by Alexis DiBiasio.

The vodka gulp game crapped out when someone got hepatitis and blamed Michael. When the hepatitis accusation became public a couple of hundred clubbers collectively freaked out over the possibility that they too might be infected. To both alleviate and aggravate the dread, at the Party Monster's instigation we published a Wheel of Hepatitis chart in our magazine Project X with arrows and lines connecting all the possible infection points. Unfortunately, our joke wasn't so relevant by the time Project X was published because we often had financial struggles that delayed our print dates by weeks and sometimes months. What was meant to be humorous and horrifying was passé. Still, all our friends pored through the chart to see if they were important enough to have had the viral vodka in their mouths.

While the infected vodka bottle might not seem relevant to spangles, it is. What mattered most about the spangles was not so much that they make a shimmering statement, but that they leave a lasting impression. So that last vision the infected nightclubbers had before contracting hepatitis? It was a band of spangles around a depraved—yet sparkly— wrist forcing the end of a vodka bottle down their throats.

# 10 CRYSTAL METH ROCK

"I remember when rock was pure
icy sparkle had much allure.
Crushing up, snorting white stones
had a mortar and pestle and a straw of my own.
But the biggest kick I ever got
was doing a thing called the crystal meth rock.
While the other kids were baking Special K
I was grinding and bopping to the crystal meth rock."

At some point while shopping in the discount fabrics district I found a children's print emblazoned with the words "crocodile party." Those words made me think of Elton John's song "Crocodile Rock." The song led to thoughts of crystal meth and rock cocaine, the good kind that is really flaky and has a beautiful mother-of-pearl luminescence before it's crushed.

It's pointless to self-analyze why my mind linked "Crocodile Rock" to cocaine or crystal meth rocks.. It just did. For better or worse (usually for better), there were lots of drugs in the clubs we frequented, especially cocaine. So it was often on my mind. If an innocent fabric could make a druggy reference, all the better. The reality, though, was that nobody got the druggy reference except me.

In fact, if the words crocodile party referenced anything, they sounded like a party Michael Alig might have thrown in the basement of the Tunnel with a cheap child's swimming pool half-filled with water mixed with spilled drinks. The crocodile party outfit on page 30 was perfect for this plausible party. It essentially was a bathing suit that shouldn't get wet because it was made of cotton broadcloth that might shrink.

Tailoring was important for a broadcloth ensemble

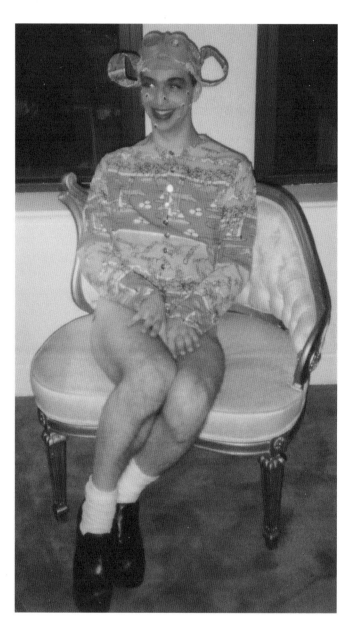

Michael Alig wears a jumpsuit and matching hat by Ernie Glam. Photo by Ernie Glam.

because the fabric didn't stretch. I had two basic patterns for the Party Monster's body. One set for fabric that didn't stretch and another for fabric that did.

The photo on page 30 suggests that the Party Monster's outfit doesn't cover his naughty parts so he's modestly covering them. However, there was a tapered bottom that covered his crotch and continued to taper to an end between his scrotum and anus. At the end were attached two straps made out of the same fabric that worked like a jock strap, coming over the ass cheeks. The end of the straps had buttonholes that fastened to buttons sewn to the back of the garment near the sides of his waist. For urination he had two options. He could either unbutton the front buttons in the fly area or he could unfasten the back buttons and lift up the front of the garment. Unbuttoning the front fly was easier when standing in front of a urinal because it didn't require holding fabric out of the urine stream's way.

But for shock value the back buttons were eventually unfastened and the Party Monster just walked around the club trying to force people to touch his junk.

# 11 GAMES OF CHANCE

The Party Monster took many risks when it came to bad behavior. Few of them resulted in him getting caught and fewer had any significant consequence, so during his rise to prominence in the club scene his behavior became more brazen.

His affinity for risk inspired the one-piece jumper on page 33. It was made of a black and white cotton-poly knit decorated with dice, appliqués and an zippered playing card crotch for easy urination. Michael took matching leftover scraps of fabric from the sewing table and tied bows on his shoes to coordinate the look. The square-front neckline was designed to expose the nipples for a louche touch. As was the case with other looks I designed for him, the goal was to be pretty, yet vulgar.

This costume interpreted risk as games of chance involving dice and playing cards. Take your life in your hands and throw some dice. Essentially the Party Monster was doing that every week at his parties. He took pills, snorted powders, drank liquor and then let the toxic elements reveal a winning or losing combination on the giant craps table that was the nightclub's dance floor. We were all placing bets on the rolls of the dice, hoping that we'd win. Mostly we did, though there were plenty of clubbers who didn't and ended up outside the club sitting on the sidewalks and vomiting while worried or annoyed friends rubbed their backs.

Rolling the dice meant snorting a white power the Party Monster told you was cocaine and then discovering that you'd in fact snorted Special K; not a stimulant, but a tranquilizer. As the dice continued rolling down the craps table, you were going down, down into the K hole. Did you win or did you lose your purse? Not sure? Roll again.

Michael Alig wears jumpsuit by Ernie Glam. Photo by Michael Fazakerley.

The playing card crotch held another surprise. Ask the dealer to hit you and what would you be dealt? Instead of getting that drink ticket that might have been designed to look like the queen of diamonds, you get Alig's sticky, flaccid cock in your hand. Did you win or did you lose? Not sure? Play another hand. Want an ace in your hole? It's behind the zipper.

The Party Monster's games of chance didn't have any fixed rules. They were subject to change according to his whims, so that nightclubbers wouldn't be sure if they had a winning hand. Was the winning hand coke and special K or Xanax and alcohol? Which combo added up to 21? Nobody was told because nobody knew. And if you were a winner, exactly what would you win? A free drink? Sex with a hottie? Admission to the VIP lounge? Like in real casinos, the big winner was the house, which raked in tens of thousands of dollars a night. What the clubbers "won" was a smile, a memory or memory lapse, a new girlfriend or boyfriend, a night of happy dancing. Everything but the jackpot, which was reserved for the club owners stuffing huge stacks of bills into money bags.

# 12 RESENTFUL OF ROYALTY

The Party Monster had, and still has, a jealous streak. He was attracted to talented people, but he also resented their abilities.

For example, I initially didn't understand the Party Monster's joking hostility that he harbored for the band Deee-lite, the dance music act that sprung out of the New York City nightclub scene in 1990 with their fabulous debut album "World Clique." Especially when it came to the band's lead singer, Lady Miss Kier, he often cracked mean jokes.

Another example is in the photograph on page 37, which captures the Party Monster's not-so-feigned resentment of one of his closest friends, the author and nightclubber James St. James. Michael was schizophrenic when it came to people who made him feel inferior. At times the Party Monster fawned over people he thought were more fabulous than he. But he also tried to bring them down a notch by making bitchy comments or pranking them.

James St. James wears his King of New York costume on page 37. The King and Queen of New York event was a scheme to get all the outlandish and popular people in the nightclub business to come to the Limelight and compete to become nightlife royalty. Some clubbers sucked up to the Party Monster in hopes that he'd rig the "election" in their favor, but many stylish queens didn't have to kiss ass.

James St. James fell halfway between a needy courtesan and aloof princess. He was one of the first club kids, a self-made celebutante who used a trust fund, free time, writing talent and a drug habit to become a demimonde star. Despite boasting about his wealth, he was often penniless and frequently needed the Party Monster's jobs.

That's how Michael got the upper hand. He hired James to make him beholden. What better way to lord over someone who makes you feel inadequate? That strategy worked. James was rather lazy in the early 1990s, so he tolerated humiliation for a paycheck.

See a glint of resentment in the Party Monster's comical expression on page 37 as he offered his friend a Judas kiss? In fact, the Party Monster is cringing at his counterpart's ability to assemble crazy, complex looks. The Party Monster's arched pinky finger finished the statement broadcast by his facial expression: He is so jealous that he barely wants to touch the arm of the legendary King of New York, someone whose style he covets.

Menswear was a target of our subversion. One favored technique was taking pre-made shirts and tarting them up with spangles and spandex panels to make them skin tight. The looks started by buying cheap men's shirts sold in the low-rent discount stores on 14th Street in Manhattan, where a man's shirt might cost $8.99. The shirts were essentially disposable, so if they were ruined after one wild night, it was no big deal.

The white dress shirt worn by the Party Monster on page 37 has elastic side panels. Making a dress shirt stretchy required cutting out the fabric at the sides and replacing it with a smaller amount of cotton spandex, which cost $1 a yard in some of the discount fabric stores in the Garment District. The elastic made the man's shirt more feminine and form-fitting.

We combined that shirt with printed cotton pique shorts that had a high, lace-up waistline. The lace was a black ribbon printed with small white polka dots. It was a fey-boy look ideal for falling down a rabbit hole into Wonderland.

James St. James, left, and Michael Alig, who is wearing a shirt and shorts by Ernie Glam. Photo by Michael Fazakerley.

# 13 LURING DISCO DOLLIES

One reason the Party Monster's events were so popular is that they gave freaks from all over the country a space to appear as they wanted to be perceived, whether that was a naked old man in a see-through negligee and tiara or a college student in a sequined diaper.

The cotton-lycra jumpsuit on page 39 was inspired by the idea of a 1920s Ziegfeld Follies showgirl gone wrong or a young ingenue lured into a life of vice by unscrupulous club owners. Or imagine a young man who came to New York City with wild expectations of breaking into show business, only to be seduced on casting couches and plied with ecstasy and special K. Once hooked on glamor, drugs and open bars, the hapless clubber spiraled into a life of party promotion, luring more ingenues from the hinterlands to the greedy club owners' lairs, where they would be swindled out of their cash and induced to dance on go-go stands for drink tickets. The plot just described was the show performed weekly at the Limelight's Disco 2000 party, and sometimes there was a line around the block to get in!

The stars in the spectacle of ingenues-gone-wild celebrated feathers, and so did the outfit on page 39. The one-piece garment had a detachable feather boa bustle supported by wires that connected to straps hidden inside the garment. The visual effect was gravity-defiance because there was no obvious structure keeping the bustle above Michael's ass.

Feathers were everywhere at Disco 2000, whose mascot was a chicken. The drag queens usually kept it classy with tasteful feather boas slung casually around their shoulders, but not knotted or gathered in front lest their fake busts be hidden. No need to hide breasts in a club full of so many

Michael Alig wears a bodysuit with a
feather bustle by Ernie Glam. Photo by
Ernie Glam.

horny young straight boys.

The club kids were more creative with feathers. Many glued them on their faces. Others on their bodies or around their nipples. At one point I glued feathers all over the Party Monster's cock so that you'd see something dangling. I envisioned the naughty appendage as the Mesoamerican feathered serpent god Quetzalcoatl, but high nightclubbers might have perceived it as a mutant New York City pigeon begging for crumbs of attention.

I even glued feathers on Clara the Carefree Chicken, Disco 2000's mascot "kidnapped" from a costume store and pressed into weekly servitude dancing in a cage above the dance floor. The stolen costume was actually made from yellow fake fur and there wasn't a single feather on it. Clara was a pretend bird, so I performed an intervention to drag-up her look. My fowl therapy consisted of gluing sequins for lipstick and feather eyelashes on Clara's giant, papier-mâché head. The decoration feminized Clara, making her face less mannish and ungainly. The added pizazz seemed to stimulate the fake furry beast. She took to Limelight's stage and danced more gracefully post-feather application, as if her inner diva were unleashed. Clara's bodysuit was machine washable, a must because by the end of every Wednesday night it reeked of sweat, body odor, cigarettes and spilled drinks.

Clara's facial glitz didn't last long. After a few months, eyelash feathers slowly dislodged and fell to the dance floor, trampled by foot-high platform sneakers. The sequined lipstick slowly fell off too, in time leaving Clara's face a busted mess not so different from the transvestites and transexuals who'd arrive at Disco 2000 around 3 a.m. after a night of turning tricks at the Meat Market District. Some of the trannies arrived with cracked foundation and smudged eyeliner. Like Clara, they just needed a drink or two by that point.

# 14 LOVING THE ALIEN

The first time I saw Leigh Bowery was in 1987 or 1988 in the basement of the Tunnel nightclub where he attended a party organized by the club kids. He was wearing one of the several babydoll dresses he brought with him on that trip with low-cut necklines that pushed up his blubber to make it look like breasts. That's a trick many of the New York City drag queens also used. One way of doing it is taking duct tape and tightly wrapping it around the lower chest just below the nipples so that the tape pushes up the fleshy parts of the pectoral muscles or the body fat that sits on top of the muscles. With a little make-up shading and contouring the look is very convincing, though this trick doesn't really work for skinny bitches.

The trick worked very well on Leigh Bowery, who didn't need the duct tape because he had ample man boobs. All he needed to do was have the dress tight just below the nipples and all his flesh plumped up like risen dough. At one point he admitted that it wasn't particularly comfortable and at times the tight fit cut into his flesh. That didn't matter to him since bleeding sores from extreme garments were just occupational hazards for a man who pierced his cheeks so he could safety-pin plastic lips to his face.

We didn't speak that first night I saw him in the basement of the Tunnel, though, because I was too intimidated to approach him. I'd seen him in the magazine i-D and even saved that i-D issue where's he's on the cover dressed like a pig. In addition to the babydoll dress, he had a head harness with two illuminated incandescent light bulbs attached near the ears. He spun on the dance floor cheerfully to the Pet Shop Boys' "You Are Always on My Mind," while I stared with incredulous pleasure.

Leigh Bowery, left, with Michael Alig, who is wearing a bodysuit by Ernie Glam. Photo by SKID.

A subsequent night I saw him at The World nightclub where we finally spoke. He explained the light-bulbs on the ears and how they burned his head, but his commitment to the look was more important than comfort or permanent scars, which he could just cover up with make-up. Both Michael Alig and I were so amused and impressed by Leigh Bowery that a few years later when we worked at the Limelight nightclub we resolved to have the wildest parties for him. At one point we invited him to a crazed dinner party inspired by one of the parties in the Russ Meyer film "Beyond the Valley of the Dolls." The party was in our apartment at W. 30th Street and food was served, but goal was to get Leigh Bowery really fucked up just for fun. At one point we ostentatiously took an eight ball of cocaine, crushed it up as all the guests watched and made dozens of lines on the fanciest plate we owned. The plate was then passed around the room until all the powder was gone. A few years later Leigh Bowery told me how much he loved our party with the fancy cocaine plate, though I was never sure if he was really sincere with anything he said because he had a teasing lilt to his speech.

Bowery's make-up, body gear and costumes had a huge effect on all the New York City nightclubbers. In the photo  on page 42, Leigh Bowery's influence is distinctly visible in the fabric I chose for Michael's body suit, which was made of a cotton-lycra knit. My unitard's floral print is similar to the print on Bowery's costume even though I probably hadn't seen Bowery's costume at the time I designed Alig's. All the New York club kids loved Bowery, and to one degree or another we were inspired by him.

# 15 INSTANT SHOW

You've paid a freaky cult celebrity thousands of dollars to fly from London and appear at your party, and the celebrity shows up in an outfit expecting to do nothing more than have a few cocktails before getting paid.

That was the Party Monster's quandary when he hired the British freak Leigh Bowery to make an appearance at Disco 2000. As the photo on page 45 illustrates, Leigh Bowery showed up in a giant, white, padded bodysuit that slightly resembled the 1960s children's television claymation character Gumby. This nocturnal version was decidedly less wholesome, with the giant words A CUNT emblazoned on his "face."

The Limelight nightclub's owner Peter Gatien expected something for the thousands of dollars he shelled out to fly Leigh Bowery to New York and put him up in a hotel. The boss expected a show. Ever the charlatan, Michael Alig assured our boss that there was indeed a wonderful show in the works, something clubbers would discuss days afterwards. The reassurances placated the boss, but there was still the unresolved question of what the performance would be. When the lightbulb finally lit up inside Michael Alig's mind, he reached for the nearest lightbulb. In this photograph there is a lamp under his arm, probably taken from our living room on W. 30th Street. The solution to the problem was that Leigh Bowery's performance would consist of screwing a lightbulb into the lamp.

So at some point during the night Great Britain's biggest freak was ordered to climb atop a platform above the bar in the Limelight's rear chapel. Of course there wasn't anything as convenient as a step ladder to help the morbidly obese alien climb on to the platform. So after a few failed, clumsy efforts the toast of London's freakdom hauled his fat ass on to the platform. Somehow there was

Leigh Bowery, left, with Michael Alig, center, and Dave Mooney. Both Michael and Dave wear jumpsuits by Ernie Glam. Photo by Alexis DiBiasio.

an electric outlet at the bar that allowed the lamp to be plugged in, and the show began. Leigh Bowery barely had use of his fingers because his outfit's sleeves ended in padded fingers. Still, he managed to screw the lightbulb into its socket, and as in the Book of Genesis, there was light. There was only half-hearted applause from the drunk club kids who watched the light go on, though most didn't react because they were "busy."

Michael Alig, I and many of the New York City club kids were influenced by Leigh Bowery, whose extreme style, obesity and body modification appealed to our sense of the perverse. Michael Alig often asked me to make outfits inspired by Leigh Bowery's madness, which is why there were so many bodysuits. In the photograph above I made him a bodysuit made of a cotton-polyester, striped-knit fabric. The garment zipped in the back and it was decorated with white spangles on the neckline. My then-boyfriend Dave Mooney is on the right and he's also wearing one of my creations, a cotton-lycra bodysuit decorated with red spangles on the neckline.

Both Michael and I aspired to wear the outrageous garments that Leigh Bowery brought to New York, but it just wasn't practical. Since the nightclubs were our job, there were always items to be carried, chairs to be arranged, errands that needed to be run because we couldn't rely on all our drunk friends or assistants. We couldn't come to the club in a pink straightjacket with our arms bound to our sides like James St. James. We had work to do.

# 16 BLAME THE MOTHER

A psychologist once told me that you can only blame your parents for screwing up your life until you're 18, after that it's your own fault.

I don't remember when Michael Alig introduced me to his mother, Elke Alig. It was probably around 1989 when he was hosting parties at the Red Zone, a nightclub on W. 54 Street in a converted television production studio where soap operas were once recorded. We met at some dinner party Michael threw in the Red Zone's restaurant on the second floor of the club. Elke was funny and charming like her son, but I figured something about her must have been strange or off-kilter to have produced such an eccentric offspring. Still, there was a possibility that Michael Alig's deviance, like mine, was self-invented. After all, my parents were completely normal, ordinary people. They probably didn't deserve to suffer the grief of raising a son who became an extreme queer determined to challenge all the rural Mexican values that they held dear.

It didn't take long to discover Elke's peculiarities. Just like her son, she's a complete attention-hungry baby. At no point can anyone ignore her when she's in the room. She asks questions, makes gestures, or she might just start crying so that you'll ask what's wrong. And what was wrong is that you weren't giving her enough attention. That was the first clue that somehow Elke played a role in her son's attention-whoring. It soon became clear that the Party Monster was created from the same mold.

Elke was manipulative. She is probably still manipulative, but I've avoided contact with her in recent years. Aside from crying to elicit sympathy, offers of help or a listening ear, she never hesitated bring up some woe-is-me story so that her listener would be motivated to do something she

Elke Alig, left, with Michael Alig, who is wearing a jumpsuit by Ernie Glam. Photo by SKID.

wanted. This annoying habit was particularly acute in the early years of her son's imprisonment. There were times when she'd call me sounding as if she was crying telling me that I had to help her son by sending money, food or whatever else Michael needed because she couldn't do it. There were times I sent Michael money, but in general I didn't because I felt that he deserved his punishment and prison sentence, so why should I make his punishment more pleasant by constantly sending him gifts? So I didn't and after avoiding Elke's calls she eventually stopped calling because she realized I was of no use.

The mother-son relationship was strange. At times they behaved like they didn't like each other very much and the overt hostility could be quite awkward to be around. Sometimes the hostility suddenly bubbled up and yelling would ensue. Or one of them would start crying, go in a room and slam a door. Other times Michael would make disparaging statements about her in front of others, which I'm sure caused more embarrassment for those third parties than for Elke.

The weirdest hostility I witnessed between them was during a club kid trip to Chicago. We either picked up Elke in a van on the way to Chicago or she met us there. While there Elke spent the evening with us at the club and then at the after-hours party. At some point during that evening I noticed a man her age who she brought to the after-hours, and then to a supermarket in the morning. Who knows why we needed to visit a supermarket at 7 a.m., but there must have been a good reason. By that point Elke's friend excused himself and she walked him to his car as we went into the store. On the way out of the supermarket Michael disparagingly asked her if she sucked his dick. It just came out of the blue and I was dumbstruck. I'd never heard anyone speak to their mother like that.

In the photograph on page 48 with Elke, Michael is wearing a jumper made of a cotton jersey with a floral print. The neckline has a sporty elastic collar that in our twisted minds gave the ensemble a "masculine" touch. I don't remember what Elke thought about my outfits for her son. Presumably she liked them or she was indifferent. If she had hated them she would have been quite vocal about it.

# 17 WILLING SIDEKICKS

The Party Monster had lots of sidekicks prior to his manslaughter conviction. I was one of them, but there were many others, male and female, who accompanied him while club hopping. There were advantages to running around with Michael Alig, such as free admission to clubs, free drinks and free drugs. There were also liabilities, as the Party Monster wasn't universally loved in clubland. Competing party promoters might not offer you jobs if they thought you were to close to their rival. Or maybe they denied you free cocktails, claiming that they'd run out of drink tickets moments before you showed up at their events.

Sidekicks served lots of useful purposes when nightclubbing. Before arriving at the club, they came to our house and helped Michael with make-up and outfits. During that primping time there were opportunities for actual conversation, since once arriving at the club there were few meaningful exchanges over the blaring music. It was also important to have a buddy when using drugs, since getting high alone was the fastest lane to addiction.

When it came to flirting, sidekicks were essential. If you were a gay man, then it was important to have at least one female sidekick. One trick the Party Monster used was to have his hottest female friend approach cute guys in the club and tell them that her friend likes him. Then if he expressed interest she'd reveal that her friend was a man. If that was offensive to the object of desire, he'd simply tell the woman that he wasn't interested, rather than possibly punching a gay guy delivering such a message.

One of the sidekicks was Sushi, a Japanese immigrant who arrived in the early 1990s barely able to speak English. It didn't matter to us that we didn't understand much of

Sushi Sakai, left, with Michael Alig. Michael wears a
jumpsuit by Ernie Glam. Photo by SKID.

what he said. We loved his outlandish looks. Anyway, we
didn't need to talk much while he accompanied us to
Chicago and other cities. He just had to look good.
Eventually he learned to speak English quite well and I was
pleased to discover a funny, intelligent man. But even
before the language barrier lifted, we found there was
something irresistibly charming about Sushi.

Despite the fun of being the Party Monster's sidekick, it

got tiresome because the Party Monster could be very insecure and needy. Often at his party Disco 2000 there was a point when he was drunk and threatening to kill himself because some Puerto Rican hottie wasn't interested in him. Then there was the drunken-mess game where he pretended to be so high that he needed his friends to hold him up or carry him around the club, when in fact it was all an act designed to attract more attention. Once I discovered the true nature of that game, I refused to play, even though other clubbers not privy to the game thought I was being a callous friend by not helping Michael in his "drunken" moment of need.

In the photo on page 51 with Sushi, Michael wears a bodysuit made of striped cotton jersey decorated with mother-of-pearl spangles on the neck line and a superhero logo on the chest. We were very fond of appliqués, iron-on patches and product logos. We particularly liked any branded patches that promoted a legacy product so that we could in some way defile the brand. We thought that simply wearing the brand was a product displacement. In the case of the Superman or Supergirl patch, there was a discussion before I applied it whether it represented the male or female refugee from the doomed planet Krypton. In the end it didn't matter. Disco 2000, where Skid took this picture, was a gender-bending playground, so the beholders drew their own conclusions.

# 18 THE PARTY MONSTER WANTS YOU!

Help Wanted: We are seeking highly motivated individuals with outsized senses of entitlement and importance to perform nightly for gawking, paying customers. Must like people, recreational drugs, nudity, cosmetics and eccentric fashion. Successful candidates must pay attention to detail and have superior social skills, particularly the ability to induce people to come to nightclubs on weeknights. The job requires a certain level of physical stamina, with long periods of time spent standing. Coordination is essential as potential hires must dance in confined spaces. Some accommodation can be made for claustrophobics, but applicants should expect to be confined to restricted, crowded spaces. The job may require heavy lifting, including crates of records, cases of vodka and intoxicated nightclubbers. Knowledge of CPR is a definite plus!

Applicants must move to New York City and party every night. In addition, some travel around the country may be required. Must be comfortable with appearances on television programs. Candidates are also expected to be spokesmodels for major nightclubs.

Interested individuals must come to the Limelight on Wednesday night dressed to thrill. You must then attract and keep our attention. If qualified, we will approach you with a job offer. No mailed or faxed resumes will be accepted and phone calls will not be returned.

This preceding job description wasn't something we published in the want ads, but we managed to convey these messages through various means.

After the club kids appeared on shows with Phil Donahue, Geraldo Rivera and Joan Rivers, maybe 100 club kids moved to New York City and they all cited the shows as

Michael Alig wears a jumpsuit by Ernie Glam. Photo by
Michael Fazakerley.

their inspiration for moving. That meant they believed our big lie: that we made lots of money working at the clubs, got driven around in limousines, lived in huge, luxury apartments. We didn't. Maybe the Party Monster and a handful of promoters made big money, but in general most of the club kids made $100 to $200 a night at the clubs, and they didn't work every night. That meant some of the club kids had to find day jobs, sex work or older admirers who would "sponsor" them in exchange for favors.

If the Party Monster favored you, there was a possibility of employment five nights a week, but that required a level of servitude that didn't sit well with some. Service to the Party Monster might include sticking by his side at clubs, coming to his home to help him style his hair or makeup, carrying him home at night when he was too high to walk straight, waking him up by 2 p.m. so that he could get to the office on time for important meetings or fetching him coffee and food.

The camouflage jumper the Party Monster is wearing on page 54 is made of a cotton broadcloth that did not stretch, so the fit was tailored. The outfit was an homage to—and a parody of—the first Persian Gulf War, which started around the same time Disco 2000 launched. With the nation whipped into a war frenzy by Saddam Hussein, it seemed appropriate to dress the Party Monster like a soldier. But not just any soldier. He had to be the commander in chief, so I found a sew-on patch that would stroke his insecure ego. While the Party Monster liked to portray himself as a fearless leader of the club kids, he was in fact wrought by fears that he wasn't good enough or that his parties would fail. I added a patch depicting an astronaut riding a rocket because the Party Monster truly was lost in space. He so absorbed in his own little universe that he may not have realized or cared that a war was raging.

# 19 DEAD EYES

The club kid Richie Rich moved to New York around 1991 or 1992 and we were instantly captivated by his cartoonish persona. For starters he spoke like Woody Woodpecker, as if he sucked all the helium out of a giant balloon, leaving his voice permanently altered. We also couldn't stop staring at his big pouty lips exaggerated by kabuki red lipstick. Then there were the pencil-thin eyebrows he borrowed from the silent film star Clara Bow. He also powdered his face white and decorated his cheekbones with dramatic rouge. But what was most compelling about Richie were his piercing eyes. He painted them starkly and layered multiple eyelashes above and below, giving him the appearance of a strange china doll that's come to life in a horror movie.

At one point the Party Monster decided that he wanted those eyes, so he did what he usually did with club kids whose style he coveted: he hired Richie to work at Disco 2000. Oh, and by the way, can you come over my house before Disco 2000 and do my make-up? So as with Amanda Lepore, who also often came to our apartment before Disco 2000 to help the Party Monster with his make-up, Richie began weekly visits.

The stark eyelashes were a great look for the Party Monster because they represented many visual ideals we shared. For one thing, the heavy eyelashes were gothic and the somehow invoked death because the blank stares they enabled were disturbing. The Richie Rich inspired make-up is evident in Michael Fazakerley's portrait of Michael on page 57. But unlike Richie Rich's sweet, cartoony visage, the Party Monster's version is darker. The mega-lashes were also creepy, like bugs. It was common to find druggy, bug-eyed people Disco 2000, so why not accentuate that buggy gaze with scary lashes? The lashes also satisfied the

Michael Alig wears a bolero jacket by Ernie Glam.
Photo by Michael Fazakerley.

club kid love of gender subversion. The Party Monster is a man wearing women's cosmetics, but he doesn't look like a traditional woman. He wasn't dressed like a traditional woman either.

On page 57 the Party Monster stared into space as if he had snorted the ultimate bump of special K and he was spiraling downwards. Maybe a little bit of him died that night. In fact, he actually was racing towards death and a rock bottom. It took about three to four years for him to reach a rock bottom and a death. Then he was arrested and sent to prison.

The costume I designed for him was a cotton corduroy plaid bolero jacket with tassels sewn on the collar and on the bottom hem of the jacket. The look included a pair of shorts made from the same fabric as the bolero. Call the look: girly boy goes pretty. Although the club kids spent much effort making themselves look grotesque, we also wanted to be attractive like everybody else. At times we needed to show the world that we weren't hiding deformed faces under all that clown makeup.

Like the outfit on page 57, most of the garments I made for the Party Monster were with cotton or cotton-polyester-blend fabrics for a very simple reason. We had a washer and dryer in our apartment and the cotton garments were mostly washable. Machine washability was more important in the past than today because smoking was allowed in clubs in the early 1990s. Add the scent of spilled drinks and sweaty body odor and you've got clothes that had to be sealed in plastic bags after the parties because they reeked.

# 20 OUTLAW PARTIES

Never tell the Party Monster that he can't enter a building or construction site or private property or a stranger's car. Don't tell him that a conversation is confidential. A request for privacy will get you the opposite.

Given these personality quirks, "No Trespassing" signs posted around New York City were welcome mats to Michael Alig. If anyone can enter a public space, then why go there? The spaces truly worth visiting, or invading, were those that were cordoned-off. That's the psychology behind lots of nightclubs that use doormen, ropes and security guards at the entrances to stoke the desire to enter. Once inside nightclubs, many partiers discover there are other restricted areas that only a privileged few can enter. That creates additional desires to penetrate restricted areas.

Outlaw parties took that psychology and added a touch of criminality. Outlaw parties were originally conceived in the mid-1980s by a club promoter named Vito Bruno, but eventually Michael Alig appropriated them and they became associated with club kids and mayhem. The outlaw parties were often held in public spaces like parks, but the best outlaw parties combined mayhem with danger. That was the recipe for an outlaw party on a section of what is today New York City's world-famous High Line. In the early 90s the High Line was a derelict railroad fenced off for the public's safety. The only people who entered the High Line were the homeless or city workers charged with shooing them out. One night while walking near Tenth Avenue and 30th Street, we noticed a fence gate whose flimsy chain and lock had been broken. That discovery immediately called for an inspection of the premises, which led to the decision to have a party there.

The funny thing about this particular outlaw party is that it

Michael Alig, left, wears a jumpsuit by Ernie Glam. Ernie Glam, right, wears a face harness and overalls he designed. Photo by David Hurley.

lasted too long. It lasted so long that I recall running out of vodka. We weren't visible to the police up on that railroad, and there wasn't the constant foot and vehicular traffic by Tenth Avenue and W. 30th Street around 1992 like in 2018. I'm not sure, but we might even have called the police to come break it up. In any case, once the liquor ran out, everybody wanted to go to the club for more drinks, so all the partiers got free passes to the Limelight. That was exactly the point of the outlaw party.

In the photo on page 60 we were at the High Line outlaw party, where Michael wore the same outfit he wore on page 51 with the club kid Sushi. This photo was taken on a different night because his lipstick is messier for the outlaw party. Since we lived together at the time, I was often recruited to help him pour liquor or carry cases of vodka into the forbidden zones. The photo on page 60 shows off Michael's ensemble's hot-pink crotch and matching feather cuffs. I also made the overalls and the face strap that I'm wearing. It was hard to see from the photographer's angle, but that was a sequined monocle attached to the face strap hovering over one of my eyes.

Readers will soon have a visual aid for imagining an outlaw party on the High Line. The section of the railroad where our outlaw party was held is now called The Spur by The Friends of the High Line, the group that led the railroad's transformation into a park. The Spur is located between Tenth and Eleventh avenues and it is expected to open as the High Line's latest phase in 2018.

Perhaps the public will find a club kid ghost on the High Line once The Spur opens. The best time to find a club kid ghost will be when the High Line begins hosting dance parties on The Spur. Search for a plastic cocktail cup crushed on the ground during one of those parties and gaze into the distorted plastic.

# 21 KING OF THE CLUBS

Is it accurate to call Michael Alig the king of the club kids?

He seemed to think of himself that way. That self-designation, along with his clever ability to get clubs to hire him as a party promoter, worked in his favor. He was the king because he often behaved most inappropriately and faced no consequences in the realm he thought he controlled. Like any king, he could ask any number of courtiers to do his bidding and they would respond accordingly. It didn't hurt that he had a nightclub's budget at his disposal to pay his courtiers.

At times he behaved like the allegedly depraved Roman emperor Caligula, whose name he appropriated for social media after his release from prison in May 2014. For instance, at a party in the basement of the Tunnel nightclub he promised everyone who came to the event that he would give them free ecstasy pills at an appointed hour. When the time came for the distribution, he got on the little stage in the club's basement and began holding the pills above the partiers' heads. He taunted the assembled guests, who all clambered over each other in their effort to score the X. As elbows flew, outfits, wigs and make-up were mussed in the frantic crush for the happy pills. Throughout the chaos Michael smiled like a maniacal Cheshire Cat, relishing every moment of humiliation he heaped on the begging crowd. As if feeding a flock of starving pigeons, he carefully tossed each pill like a bread crumb to the desperate horde.

A similar experience at the Red Zone was his Diving for Dollars parties, where he tossed dollar bills from a terrace. The frenzied crowd below scrambled for a pittance while the hypocritical tyrant above feigned generosity for his destitute subjects.

Michael Alig wears a vest and shorts by Ernie Glam. Photo by
Michael Fazakerley.

Like a king, he was surrounded by people who laughed at his jokes, until the joke was on them. I remember one assistant who Michael even kicked and punched when he was drunk, and that clubber always forgave his majesty and came back. Mostly the abused club kid kept returning because he didn't have any other job options, or getting occasionally abused by the king was easier to stomach than a day job requiring hard work.

What didn't work in his favor was his imperious attitude that grew more obnoxious as we became more addicted to drugs. That meant challenging authorities like police officers if they were trying to stop the club kids from having a riot at the corner donut shop. If the confrontations with authorities resulted in an arrest, all the better for it burnished his highness' cred as an outlaw. The king also loved to make people wait, and wait, by never arriving on time. In the recent and distant past, he'd make me wait hours. Despite my anger, I eventually forgave him. And then I waited some more.

I made both the blue vest and mauve shorts Michael was wearing on page 63, but they were not originally made as one ensemble. The shorts were made of cotton corduroy and they had a matching bolero jacket. The royal blue vest was made of microsuede. I chose gold buttons for the vest because I liked Edwardian fashion and dandies. The gold buttons paired with the vest's royal blue fabric was something I imagined Oscar Wilde would wear while having some risqué conversation in a Parisian cafe about sleazy sex with a drunk British sailor

# 22 KING & QUEEN OF NEW YORK

Almost every year the Party Monster worked at the Limelight he threw his King & Queen of New York party. One year, either in 1992 or 1993, he asked me to be one of the contenders for the King of New York. I agreed to let him put my name on the list, even though I was certain that I wouldn't win. I suspected that the Party Monster had already chosen a winner, although he always denied that the event was rigged.

The event required a new outfit because many attendees took the contest seriously and turned themselves out. Some might have hoped that they'd be plucked from the club's audience and nominated. Others probably dressed their best to upstage the official candidates. In any case, these events brought out the pageant in many of us. For this night I made the Party Monster a cotton-lycra white body suit with stars and a matching, detachable cape lined with black satin and trimmed with pink feathers. The idea for the look on page 66 was a royal audience with the king and queen. That meant a cape of some sort.

The King and Queen of New York competition had a panel of judges that the Party Monster usually chose. In general he'd choose people who for him represented the club "royalty" of the 1980s. For this particular event his choices included the writers Michael Musto and George Wayne, the photographer Marcus Leatherdale and Larissa, a French woman and party hostesses who represented the Euro-trashy crowds that 1980s mega-clubs coveted. The Party Monster lionized these people because their acceptance of his invitation to judge was a validation by the previous generation of nightclub dignitaries. The Party Monster fawned over these people, plying them with drinks and attending to all their needs. That deference became the bullseye for the prank I sprang on Michael and

Michael Alig wears a bodysuit by Ernie Glam. Photo by
Michael Fazakerley.

and judges during the contest.

Once the Limelight was full, the music on the main dance floor stopped and the competition began. George Wayne moderated the event and introduced the contenders, who I can't remember. I also can't remember what I wore, though it may have had guerrilla influences. My matching accessory was a giant Super-Soaker squirt gun. During the contest George Wayne handed the microphone to the contestants, who'd promise the audience how they'd be sweet, glittering overlords of the club realm. They were similar to Miss America speeches, except with drug and sex innuendoes.

When it was my turn George Wayne handed me the microphone and I walked to the end of the runway. Then I began a tirade that I vaguely remember as:.

"Who are these self-appointed arbiters of fabulousness? Why should it matter what they think? I say we reject them and be free."

In the middle of the rant I walked back to the center of the stage near the judges, aimed my Super-Soaker at them and unleashed a torrent of plain water, not urine or any other noxious liquid. The judges at first just sat there, trying to swat the water away. I particularly aimed for Larissa's face, which was always caked with foundation and black eye-liner plus eye shadow. From the corner of my eye I noted that George Wayne, who wasn't at the judge's table because of his hosting duties, was giggling and stomping his feet with laughter. About 20 seconds after shooting the judges I handed the microphone to George Wayne and walked off the stage. As I was almost off the stage Marcus Leatherdale threw either a glass or beer bottle at me. It missed, but I thought his reaction was disproportionately violent. All I did was squirt him with water and he threw something that could have caused serious injury.

After my outburst the Party Monster was furious. I had embarrassed and disrespected his venerated guests in front of the entire club. Now his esteemed dignitaries were angry at him for permitting such a spectacle and he was apologizing profusely to them. I had pranked the Party Monster and there would be repercussions. I didn't get any drink tickets that night and there was a short-lived silent treatment. I don't believe I apologized to the judges for soaking them at the party of afterwards. I meant them no ill will and my prank was just a surprise joke designed to get a laugh out of the audience. Michael Musto always greets me and chats when we see each other, so I guess he forgave me. I've never seen or spoken with Larissa or Marcus Leatherdale since then. If either Larissa or Marcus read this, my apologies.

# 23 MEDIA HOAX

As a child I was fascinated by the public reaction to the broadcast of "War of the Worlds." The 1938 radio show allegedly frightened listeners who thought that the drama was an actual newscast reporting an alien invasion. The misperception surrounding the event began my interest in media hoaxes, particularly those perpetrated by P.T. Barnum, the 19th-century circus and sideshow impresario.

After meeting the Party Monster, a real life P.T. Barnum, the possibility of committing our own media hoax became a reality. That hoax culminated in the club kids.

My participation in the hoax began in 1989 at the Red Zone nightclub. The Party Monster had hired me to go-go dance at his Saturday night Cabaret Revoltaire party. He paid me $75 to stand on the bar for a few hours dressed in a crazy outfit while I got drunk from the handful of drink tickets he'd give each dancer. One night we were informed that a reporter from the local FOX television affiliate was coming to the Red Zone to interview us about the wild nightlife and the club kids.

Even though we were only paid $75, the Party Monster instructed us to tell FOX 5's entertainment reporter Robyn Carter that we made hundreds of dollars a night for just dressing wild and partying. With as straight a face as I could muster given the twisted pipe cleaners glued all over my upper lip, I told Robyn Carter that the wilder I looked the more money I made.

The club kid Sebastian Jr., who at the time was a student at the Fashion Institute of Technology, was also interviewed. Robyn Carter asked what his parents thought about his extracurricular activities.

"They think I'm at home studying, probably," he casually told the reporter.

To my surprise and the Party Monster's delight, the false narrative we fed the news reporter made it on to the nightly news fairly unaltered. Someone had videotaped the segment, which we repeatedly watched, each time laughing heartily over our practical joke. In July 2015 we published Robyn Carter's news report on our YouTube channel The Peeew! For ease of search we entitled the clip "Fox News seeks out the club kids."

Soon more television news crews arrived. It wasn't just word of mouth or one producer watching a competitor's newscast that brought the crews. I later learned that the Party Monster had publicists who worked at the Red Zone and at the other clubs that employed him. The publicists spun various tales about the club kids that enticed the news crews. One tall tale was that we threw parties in big trucks. Validating that myth required the Party Monster to pay a trucker to drive us around downtown so that some television crew could record us climbing into the big rig's trailer in the Meat Market District. Then the crew recorded us in a considerably disheveled condition stepping out of the trailer when it arrived at the Limelight. Even the big rig's gentle turns at corners on its 10-block trip to the Limelight nearly broke limbs as we careened uncontrollably from one side of the trailer to another because there was nothing to hold on to.

All this media attention didn't even have the negative repercussions that could have been expected. Take the time he stole the Clara the Carefree Chicken costume, along with two others, from a Manhattan costume shop. The costumes were easily worth hundred of dollars, yet the costume shop made no attempt to track them down. Even after photographs and video of the characters appeared in local newspapers and television newscasts

Michael Alig wears a bodysuit by Ernie Glam. Photo by
Michael Fazakerley.

indicating that they were mascots at the Limelight, we got no calls from an aggrieved costumer.

Another piece of the hoax was the Style Summit, an unconventional convention that we borrowed from The Rocky Horror Picture Show. Just like Dr. Frank N. Furter, we wanted to assemble a crowd of freaks from across the galaxy to show them how we party. Like many of our events, we initially thought just the New York club kids would come to the series of parties, but as we advertised the event in Project X magazine, the style magazine we published out of the Limelight, we began to receive RSVPs from around the country. Then the publicists at the Limelight began spinning their tales of how a movement of wild hedonists were having their national convention at the Limelight. Again, media outlets published stories about the Style Summit and our antics. For example, The Philadelphia Inquirer published an article about the Style Summit on the front page of their Sunday style section on May 23, 1993. The subhead stated: "This N.Y. party is outrageous, even by THEIR standards." It was another feather in our hoax's cap.

The ultimate feather was the most mainstream publication. When TV Guide published its Nov. 7-13, 1992 issue with Frank Sinatra on the cover, there was a full-page ad on page 107 for the Geraldo Show. The ad was a photograph of Sacred Boy, me, Kabuki Starshine and Keda at the Limelight. Across our photo was a question. "It's 4 a.m. Do you know where your children are?" followed by the episode's title, "Club kids: Creatures of the night." With this ad's appearance in the formerly most-read magazine in the United States, our media hoax was complete.

For a certain period the Party Monster wanted floral prints for his jumpers. He also liked pearly spangles, so in the photograph on page 71 I made a cotton-lycra low-cut bodysuit to reveal his nipples when he wanted. The ensemble also showed off his cock, which was stuffed to one side of the garment. I called it the thorn in the rosebush. Again, the idea behind this outfit was to highlight his beauty and not his perverse or repulsive nature. That idea was a hoax too.

# ABOUT THE AUTHOR

Ernie Glam, December, 2017.
Photo © by KC Mulcare.

Ernie Glam is a journalist, author, creator and nightclub personality. He moved to New York City in 1984 and for almost three years at the Limelight nightclub he portrayed Clara the Carefree Chicken, the mascot of the Disco 2000 party.

His journalism career began in 1991 at the magazine Project X. He has worked as a full-time news reporter since 1999. He previously published "69 Hangovers" in 2016 and "The Darkest Tunnel" in 2015. He currently co-hosts the YouTube comedy show The Peeew! with Michael Alig.

He was born and raised in Sacramento and graduated from the University of Pennsylvania in Philadelphia. He lives in the Bronx.

Printed in Poland
by Amazon Fulfillment
Poland Sp. z o.o., Wrocław

31566321R00045